YA FF

1773790

Published in 2007 in Great Britain by
Barrington Stoke Ltd
18 Walker St, Edinburgh, EH3 7LP

www.barringtonstoke.co.uk

ISBN: 978-1-84299-460-3

Printed in Great Britain by Bell & Bain Ltd

A Note from the Author

I've been lucky. I've never had a boyfriend who has dumped me for one of my friends. Your friends are the ones that know most about you. They know all your secrets. Losing your boyfriend to your best friend must be horrible. How can you ever forgive them – and who do you blame?

Everyone tells you that keeping your friends is more important than having a boyfriend. But when you really fancy someone, you don't make sense any more. The funny thing is, it doesn't get easier as you get older! So I wanted to write about something that really happens to people and how – in spite of what we're told to do – we don't always behave very well.

For my Wychwood girls –

you are *all* my favourites

Contents

1   Perfect Together   1

2   Hanging Out   9

3   Three's a Crowd   17

4   The Row   28

5   Nobody's Perfect   40

Chapter 1
Perfect Together

When Dan asked me out it didn't seem real. I'd been thinking about him every day and every night for weeks. Shannon and I had talked about his hair, his eyes, his style – he was perfect in every way. And he had asked *me* out! Me, Kate Carson, with the big feet and wonky nose!

When I told Shannon, she didn't say anything. For a moment she looked sad. Then she gave me a big smile and said, "Wicked!" and I knew everything was OK.

And it was. Dan was perfect. He made my life perfect. I felt perfect when I was with him. Even other people said we were perfect together.

"You are so lucky," said my younger sister Sally. "He's so fit!"

"He seems like a nice lad," said my dad. "Nice manners."

"You look very happy," said my mum.

Dan and I went everywhere together. I didn't care where – as long as he was with me I was happy.

"Let's go to the ice rink," he said one day.

"But I can't skate," I said.

"Nor can I. Do you think that's a problem?"

We bumped and giggled our way around the rink. We fell so many times. When I got home my bum was black and blue. But at the time I hadn't even felt it.

Another time he took me to a film. It was awful.

"This is crap," I muttered.

"I'm so glad you said that." He grinned at me. "I thought you were enjoying it."

"God, no. It's rubbish."

"Do you want to leave?"

I shook my head. "We've paid for the tickets. I hate leaving before the end."

"Me too. I've got an idea." He looked around the cinema. There were about 20 other people there. "Let's not watch the film. Let's watch the people watching the film."

I stared at him. "What?"

"Look." He pointed. "That boy's just dropped popcorn down that girl's top."

"And that man's fast asleep," I said.

Dan sniffed. "And what's that nasty smell?"

From then on we watched the people round us, not the film. We made up stories about them too – how the sleeping man had 16 children at home and so he came to the cinema for a bit of peace. How the popcorn couple had been going out for three days and all along he had been two-timing her. How the lady with the horrible perfume had just split up with her husband.

Lots of people gave us angry looks, and we got told to "shut up" several times, but we didn't care. We were having too much fun.

Chapter 2
Hanging Out

Shannon giggled when I told her about the cinema. "You two," she said, grinning. "What are you like?"

"I know. We're crazy."

"Yes," she agreed. "But at least you're crazy together. I don't have anyone to be crazy with."

"You've got me," I said.

"I know. But you're not always around now. Sometimes I want to be crazy and you're out with Dan."

"Well, why don't you come with us?" I said, before I could stop myself.

"Don't be stupid," she said, but her face had this kind of hopeful look.

How could I back out now? Anyway, I felt sorry for her. "I mean it. We're going to the park on Sunday. Why don't you come with us?"

So she did. And it was cool. We had a laugh. She got on really well with Dan. "She's all right," he said to me at one point. "Kind of loud but she's OK."

I smiled. "I know. She's my best friend ever. It's cool that you guys get on."

The following Friday, Dan, Shannon and I went bowling. Shannon was hopeless.

"We've been bowling before," I said. "How come you can't remember what to do?"

"Just not having any luck," she said, as her ball fell into the gutter yet again.

"It's the letting go that's wrong," said Dan. "Look. Pull your arm back, let go and then follow through."

Shannon watched him do it. "You're so good at this," she said. "Show me how to do it again."

"She's a bit dumb, isn't she?" asked Dan later. "She didn't even get it after the third time. I even had to show her how to put her fingers in the holes."

I was puzzled. Shannon was not normally this stupid. It was weird. Dan even had to hold her hands onto the ball to get her to throw it right.

As I fell asleep that night I was thinking hard. Had Shannon just been playing stupid? And if so, why?

Chapter 3
Three's a Crowd

After that, I felt I had to ask Shannon along every time Dan and I went out. If I didn't, she looked really upset. And I didn't want to lose my best friend over a boy. After all, the mags tell you that friends are more important than your boyfriend, don't they?

But as the weeks went by, I began to wish that Dan and I could have some time alone together. It wasn't that Shannon was a drag – she wasn't – but Dan and I were a *couple*. If you are a couple, don't you spend time together being romantic and all that kind of stuff?

Dan didn't understand when I talked to him about it. "Shannon's cool," he said. "It's OK if she wants to come along."

"But don't you think it would be nice to be just us?" I said.

He shrugged. "Then just tell her not to come."

So I tried. "Shannon," I said one day. "There's something I need to tell you."

"What is it?"

"It's about me and Dan," I said.

Her eyes opened wide. "You haven't split up, have you?"

I was shocked. "No, no, of course not. Why do you think that?"

She looked at the floor. "Oh, no reason."

"What do you mean? Is there something you're not telling me? Has Dan said something?"

She looked at me, and there was an odd look in her eyes. "No, it's nothing. I expect I'm being silly. Forget it. What was it you were going to say?"

But I was puzzled now. Had Dan told her he didn't like me after all? The two of them were getting on so well. Maybe he told her things that he didn't tell me?

In the end, I didn't say anything, but I was thinking up a plan.

"Let's go out for a meal somewhere," I said to Dan the next day. "Just the two of us."

"Cool," he said. "I'll choose the place."

21

I made a real effort to dress up. When I'd done my make-up, even my nose didn't look so wonky any more. "You look nice," said my sister.

Dan agreed. "You look amazing," he said, and kissed me.

The place he chose was lovely, much more posh than I expected.

"I saved up from my weekend job," said Dan.

"Wow," I said. "You're the best."

He grinned. Then I saw his eyes flicker to the door. "Oh look," he said. "It's Shannon."

"What?" I turned in my seat to look.

"Hi, you two," she said, skipping over to our table. "I just came in to say hi!"

"How did you know where we'd be?" I asked.

Shannon grinned at Dan. "Well, Dan needed a bit of help choosing where to eat, and I said it was nice here. And just think – he did what I told him!"

I turned to Dan.

"Yeah," he said. "And you were right, Shannon. This place is great! As you're here, why not join us?"

"Are you sure?" Shannon said, looking at me. I was kicking Dan under the table, but what could I say?

"Yeah, if you have to," I muttered.

"You're so sweet," she said, sitting down. "Ooh, how can I ever choose what to have from this yummy menu?"

I was furious. But what I could say? I just sat there and smiled until my face hurt. But I wanted to punch her nose to make it as wonky as mine.

Chapter 4
The Row

"I'm taking you out tonight," I told Dan the next Friday.

"Where are we going?" he asked.

"You'll see when we get there," I laughed. My mobile rang.

"Hi Kate, it's Shannon. Do you fancy coming round mine tonight?"

"Sorry, Shannon," I said. "I said I'd help my mum this evening. She wants to make a birthday cake for my dad and I said I'd ice it."

"Oh," she said. "Oh, OK. Well, see you tomorrow."

Dan was looking at me. "Why did you lie to her?" he said. "Why didn't you just tell her you were out with me?"

"She'd have wanted to come too," I said. "And I want you all to myself."

"Mmm," he said. "Sounds nice."

We had a fantastic evening. I took him to a pizza place and then to this field where we could see the stars.

"You're amazing." Dan nuzzled my ear.

I didn't know what to say, so I kissed him on the neck. I felt so happy.

But when I got home, Mum said, "Oh, Shannon called."

I felt very cold suddenly. "What did you tell her?"

"I said you were out with Dan. Why, what should I have told her?"

She's gonna kill me, I thought.

As I expected, next day Shannon was waiting for me by the school gates. She had

her arms crossed and was tapping her foot.
She looked really mad. "Well?" she snapped.

"Well what?"

"Why did you lie to me?"

"What do you mean?"

"Oh, don't play dumb." Shannon threw
her bag on the ground. "You told me you
were baking a cake with your mum. A *cake*.
Was that the best you could think of?"

"Um."

"Why didn't you just tell me you were out with Dan?"

I gave a sigh. "OK, I'm sorry," I said. It's just – I wanted to have more time with him. You know."

"What are you talking about? You're always having time with him!"

"Yes, but not – alone. Not just him and me."

Her eyes blazed. "Are you saying you don't want me around?"

"I'm not saying that! Well, sort of, but I mean – "

"No, that's fine." Shannon picked up her bag. "I understand. You don't want me showing you up. You want to be as perfect as him. Mr and Mrs Perfect. Well, you know what? He's not as perfect as you think. See you around, Kate."

And she walked off.

I stood and stared after her. What did she mean? "He's not as perfect as you think" – what was she talking about?

A cold fear swept over me. Was there something Dan wasn't telling me? Did Shannon know something about Dan? Was he cheating on me?

I don't know how I got to the end of the school day. My mind was miles away. I got told off five times for not listening. All I could think about was what Shannon had said. By the end of the day I was in a panic.

37

I called Dan as soon as I got home.

"Hi, babe," he said. "Been thinking about you all day."

"Me too," I muttered. Was he lying to me?

"Listen, my best mate's throwing a party next weekend. He's booked this cottage somewhere. It sounds really cool. We could stay over too."

"Stay over?" I said.

"Yeah." His voice went all low and soft. "I was thinking ... you know ... maybe we could ... well ..."

"Um," I said in a small, tight voice. "I'm not sure. Can I call you later?" And I hung up.

Chapter 5
Nobody's Perfect

When Mum came in I was still staring at the phone. "Are you OK?" she said.

"Mum, how can you tell if a boy really likes you? I mean *really* likes you. Not playing you along or something?"

Mum dropped her keys onto the hall table. "I'm not sure there is an answer to that. Sometimes you can see it in his eyes. But people can hide their feelings very well. I think you just have to trust your own feelings."

"But what if you're confused?"

She smiled at me. "Then the best thing to do is to cool off for a bit. Take a break. Don't see him for a while. Then you'll know how you feel about him. And you'll know how he feels about you."

"I just want things to be perfect," I said.

Mum shook her head. "Sorry, there's no such thing. Nobody's perfect."

I told Dan later that I would have to miss the party. He sounded annoyed. "I thought you'd jump at the chance. It'll be just the two of us."

"I know. I'm sorry. I just can't. Mum says I have to study. I'm behind on my school work." It was a lie.

Dan was so annoyed with me that I didn't see him for a few days. But the good thing was that I made it up with Shannon. She was really nice about the Dan problem.

"If you're not ready then you're not ready," she said. "He should understand that. Anyway, you have to trust him before you go that far with him. And I don't think you do, do you?"

I didn't know what to think any more.

On the Monday after the party weekend, a girl called Emma came up to me. "You're Kate, aren't you?" she said.

"That's right."

"Didn't you used to go out with Dan?"

"Used to? I still do," I said.

She went pink and looked confused. "Oh, sorry. I must have got it wrong."

She started to walk away. "Hey, wait a moment!" I called. "What's this all about? What's going on?"

She looked away from me. "It's nothing to do with me. I just saw him at the weekend, that's all."

"Where?"

"At this party in the country."

My heart almost stopped. He went to the party without me! "Well?"

"Well, he told everyone you'd split up. He was snogging Shannon all night." Emma took one look at my face and ran away.

Suddenly it was all clear to me. Shannon never wanted me to go out with Dan in the first place. She wanted him for herself. It was all a plan, right from the start. She never let us have time alone together. And then she started working on my mind. She made me suspect that Dan didn't like me any more

However could I fall for it? However could I think that she was my best friend? All the time she was lying to me. All the time she was working out how to get Dan for herself.

And Dan fell for it, like a total idiot. Did he ever really like me? Or was he using me to get close to Shannon? When he kissed me under the stars in that field, was he thinking of her? However could I think that we were perfect together?

I must have been blind.

Shannon was in an Art lesson. I just walked in, past the teacher and over to her table. Then I swung my right arm back and let fly. It smashed into her nose and she fell off her stool. Blood ran down her face. She'll have a wonky nose now too.

Now I'm sitting outside the Head's office, waiting to be suspended. I don't care. It will have been worth it.

Shannon, Dan, me. My mum was right after all. Nobody's perfect.

Barrington Stoke would like to thank all its readers for commenting on the manuscript before publication and in particular:

Ashleigh Crowely

Vicky Frost

Luke King

Karl McCoy

Helen McCurrach

Lee McIntosh

Rob Newman

Jordan Shaw

Billie Watson

Sean Robertson

Larrry White

Become a Consultant!

Would you like to give us feedback on our titles before they are published? Contact us at the address below – we'd love to hear from you!

Email: info@barringtonstoke.co.uk
Website: www.barringtonstoke.co.uk

More exciting NEW titles ...

Useless

by

Tanya Landman

Rob has 2 dads.

The real one – who walked out.

The stepdad – who walked in
and took Dad's place.

Who should Rob hate?

Who can Rob trust?

You can order *Useless* directly from our website
at **www.barringtonstoke.co.uk**

More exciting NEW titles ...

Stray

by

David Belbin

EVEN IN A GANG,

SHE'S ON HER OWN.

Stray's in with the wrong lot.

Can Kev save her?

Or will she drag him down?

You can order *Stray* directly from our website at
www.barringtonstoke.co.uk

More exciting NEW titles ...

Speed
by
Alison Prince

THE NEED FOR SPEED

Deb loves to drive fast.

The faster, the better.

Until she goes too far, too fast ...

You can order *Speed* directly from our website at
www.barringtonstoke.co.uk